GRIM LOVERS 3
Lilith Leana

Table of Contents

Acknowledgement

A big thank you to my husband for always believing in me and never making me feel like I couldn't do it.

Cover art

Cover art from Depositphotos

Cover design

Lilith Leana with Canva

Brief Summary

The Thief

What if Aladdin fell for another Thief instead of Princess Jasmine?

Azalea wants revenge on the Sultana for losing her job as the princess maiden. When Jafar issues a grand reward for the Sultana crown, she takes it with both hands, only to be robbed by Aladdin during the heist.

Aladdin meets a new thief on a heist and falls head over heels for the strong female who was almost quicker than him.

The Huntsman

What if the Huntsman helped Snow White defeat the Evil Queen?

Snow White's heart has been broken repeatedly by those she once trusted, leaving her feeling betrayed and alone. Placing all her faith in the Huntsman, she clings to the hope that he is deserving of her trust. When she defeats the Evil Queen, she realizes she wants more from him than just his loyalty - she craves his love.

The Huntsman helps Snow White regain her rightful throne. But the thought of witnessing her marry someone else is unbearable for him. He asks her to relieve him of his duties, but she refuses.

The Bear

What if Goldilocks fell asleep in a single man's bed?

Fleeing from her burning house, Goldilocks stumbled upon an open door. She falls asleep in a soft bed, only to be rudely awakened by the disgruntled owner. She apologizes and wants to make things right so she can stay in his bed.

When Bjorn Beren finds a pretty girl in his bed he is furious at first, but as he gets to know her he can't wait to get her back in his bed, naked.

The Mad Hatter

What if Alice returned to Wonderland as an adult?

Alice has been searching for the entrance of Wonderland ever since she returned to England. When she finds it, she immediately falls into the arms of her long-lost love, the Mad Hatter.

The Mad Hatter almost doesn't believe that Alice is truly back in his arms, but now that he has her again, he never wants to let go.

Bluebeard

What if the Little Mermaid found love with Bluebeard?

The Little Mermaid traded her Siren voice for legs, but gets betrayed by the man who she did it for. Desperate to escape her fate, she stands on top of a cliff only to be rescued by another lone soul, Bluebeard.

Bluebeard, who is also surrounded by a curse, is there to save Ariel and free her with a true love's kiss when she almost loses her life a second time by magic.

READER ADVISORY: THIS story contains explicit sex scenes.

Grim Lovers 3 is a collection of five previously published standalone short erotic stories.

It is filled with your favorite fairytale retellings. Explicit sex scenes, standalone, no cheating or cliffhangers.

The Thief

What if Aladdin fell for another Thief instead of Princess Jasmine?

I wanted the Sultana crown more than anything in my life. Not just for the reward that Jafar had issued, but for revenge. I had lost my job as the princess maiden when she married that magical man. Who needed a helping hand when your husband could just conjure everything he wanted? But more than a job, I had also lost my friend.

I was perfect for the heist since I knew every inch of the castle, having grown up and worked there my whole life until the marriage. The resentment burned hot in my veins and fueled my desire for revenge. I might not have the most experience in stealing, but I knew how to get in and out of any room without being seen. People never paid attention to a servant, anyway.

With no trouble, I got into the throne room, and I had my hands on the crown when he appeared. Another thief. Aladdin. He was too handsome for this line of business, but his hands were quick and nimble. I grabbed the crown before it could disappear into his robes, but his hand covered mine.

"This is mine, Princess," he whispered.

"I'm no Princess," I answered.

"I know. You're a thief. Just like me," Aladdin said with a wink.

Before I could give a tart reply, the door of the throne room opened, and he pulled me behind the curtains. His muscular body pushed mine against the wall, our hands still locked together on the golden crown.

I slid out my knife from its holster, holding it against his neck. He had the audacity to smirk. Why did he have to be so handsome? I studied his features closer as the footsteps of the guards echoed through the room. His dark hair was a tad too long and almost covered his gorgeous brown eyes. They glittered with mischief, and his supple lips were curved in a smirk. His nose was too big for his face, but his sharp jawline evened it out. His masculine, intoxicating smell filled my senses and when our eyes met, I could feel something spark inside of me.

"Don't you love the thrill of a heist? The change of getting caught?" Aladdin whispered as the sounds of the guards doing their rounds came closer.

Any moment now they would pass us by and if they looked too close to the curtain, they would see our feet below. As the adrenaline coursed through my veins, I could feel the excitement bubbling up inside me. I didn't want to give him the satisfaction of agreeing with him. I was nothing like him. I did this out of revenge because I had a point to make and granted the royal sum Jafar had promised.

Aladdin saw this kind of thing as a sport or a hobby. He didn't even need it to sustain himself. He gave most of his bounty away to the less fortunate. Which also made him more likable. But I didn't want to like him. He was my rival, and we were both after the same thing. I clutched the crown harder, aware that he would take it from me the moment my attention slipped.

His massive body pushed closer to me, trying to occupy the small space we had to avoid being discovered. Lust filled his eyes as something between us hardened.

"Are you getting aroused now?" I asked, as anger burned through my veins.

"As if you aren't. The prize is in your hands. You have a knife at my throat. You have the upper hand in this equation. Admit that you're as turned on as I am."

I opened my mouth to say something. I didn't know if I was going to admit or deny his accusation, but his free hand covered my lips. Naked skin against my mouth. On instinct, I bit his palm, and a groan escaped him. His taste, salty and intense, overwhelmed my senses as adrenaline coursed through me.

The footsteps came closer, and our breathing sped up. He bent his head lower, his mouth so close to my ear that I could feel his warm breath fanning my face, his intoxicating smell enveloping me.

"The first rule of being a thief, Princess, is not making a sound," Aladdin whispered in my ear.

A shiver passed through me as he slowly ground his hips against mine, pushing his hard cock against my pussy. The footsteps passed us by, and I had to hold back the urge to bite him again. He lifted his hand from my mouth, lingering his fingers on my lips. I opened my mouth, letting my tongue out to play, tasting him again.

"I'm no Princess," I growled against his fingers.

My grip tightened around the crown when I felt he moved it higher above our heads. He gently placed it on my head, startling me with the heavy weight of it.

"But you look so good wearing a crown," Aladdin whispered before his mouth covered mine.

I moaned into the kiss, my hands grabbing his shoulders to keep me steady, my knife loose in my hand, almost forgotten. He pushed me up against the wall, parting my legs to make room for his hips. Before I knew what was happening, he was rubbing his cock against my pussy, igniting pleasure as his tongue played with mine.

One of his hands slid in between us, underneath my robes, seeking out my aching pussy. I really should have told him to stop, but it felt so good. When his hand reached my wet pussy, he groaned into my mouth. The guards had passed us, but soon they would discover that the crown was gone. His lips left mine as his fingers circled my clit, making pleasure rise.

"Such a little liar. You're sopping wet."

"Shut up," I growled.

Before I could say more, he rubbed my clit harder, sparking pleasure inside of me and effectively shutting me up. I bit his neck to muffle the sounds of my pleasure, making him tremble against my body. I could feel his cock become even harder against me, and I knew he was aching for a release as well. Maybe after this was all over and I delivered the crown to Jafar, I could pay Aladdin another visit to finish this in the best way.

My thoughts scrambled when his movements became more urgent. We didn't have much time before the guards would sound the alarm, and it seemed that Aladdin was determined to pull an orgasm out of me before that happened. His finger circled my clit, sparking pleasure with each move. My legs trembled, only held up by his muscular body against mine.

The footsteps halted, and I could hear muffled voices. My breathing quickened, and I could feel my heartbeat speed up as my pleasure grew. A few more strokes and then my orgasm washed over me. My pussy clenched around nothing as pleasure filled my senses. I bit my lip hard to keep my sounds of pleasure muffled. Aladdin looked at me, lust and determination fighting for a place. Before I could understand what was happening, my feet were on the ground and my hands were bound with the curtain rope.

My body was still trembling with my release when Aladdin whispered. "Second rule of being a thief. Never take your eyes off your target."

With a wink, he was gone, taking the crown and my knife with him. It only took me a moment to get free, but he was long gone and I had to shake off the guards who had finally noticed the crown missing.

A few days later, I found his hideout, and I was waiting for him in the dark. When he came in, I tackled him, holding my new knife to his throat.

"You owe me an orgasm and a crown, Aladdin."

He held his hands up in surrender and smirked that stupid delicious mouth of his. "I can't give you a crown, but I can double the orgasm."

"Where is it?" I asked, but before I could get answers out of him, he rolled us over, took my knife from me, and pinned me down on the ground.

I struggled with all my might, but his weight was too much for me to move. My struggling only resulted in my legs widening and his cock hardening against me. I should not be getting aroused by this filthy thief on top of me, but his husky scent and his firm body did things to me I couldn't control.

"Jafar stole it from me, Princess. But if we work together, I'm sure we can get it back."

I didn't trust him as far as I could throw him, but I knew I couldn't deal with Jafar alone. With a sigh, I let myself relax in his grip, hoping to catch him off guard.

"Okay, we will work together. Now get off me."

He cocked his head to the side, a whisk of dark hair falling across his forehead, and he smirked. "But I like you underneath me, Princess."

"My name is Azalea," I gritted through my teeth as I bucked my hips trying to get him off me, but it only nestled his hard cock against my pussy.

"Azalea," he said, savoring my name as if it was his favorite drink in the world. A shiver passed through me, and I could feel arousal starting to rise. "Does this count as foreplay?" Aladdin asked as he leaned in closer until our lips were a hair's breadth apart, and I could smell his tantalizing breath. "I still owe you two orgasms, I believe."

I bridged the distance between our lips, kissing him with all the anger and frustration that I felt. Two orgasms might be a good way to get all of that out, and after we could focus on getting the crown back. His tongue met mine, and I moaned when his taste filled my senses. It was a mix of black tea and sweet dates that shouldn't be so delicious as it was. I wanted to savor the kiss since I hadn't had a chance before, but Aladdin didn't let me. In one move, he turned us over again, letting me straddle him.

"You look good on top of me, Pr- Azalea," he said.

His saying my name with his husky voice should not be as hot as it was. With a curse, I kissed him again, tugging at his clothes, trying to get to his naked skin. I uncovered his chest and moaned when I saw his hard muscles covered in a thin trail of hair leading me to his pants. He was absolutely ripped, but not in an overly muscular way. His body was built like that of a thief, strong and nimble, but not massive.

"Liking what you see?" Aladdin asked, one eyebrow lifted.

"Shut up," I said and kissed him.

I didn't want to give him the satisfaction of admitting that I was attracted to him, but my body betrayed me. He ripped away the fabric of my top, and my nipples hardened immediately, begging to be touched by him. His hands were surprisingly soft as they covered my breasts. My back arched involuntarily, pressing my aching breasts harder in his hands as I made a soft sound full of need.

"But I like your reaction to my words. You're so easily annoyed by me," Aladdin said.

I rolled my eyes and tried to push him away, but his mouth dove down, closing around one of my nipples. This was a way better use of his mouth, anyway. His nimble tongue circled around my nipple, sucking it in his mouth until it was hard and aching. Arousal coursed through me as his tongue and mouth worked my breast. When he was happy with the first one, he switched to my other breast and gave it the same treatment.

My hands were in his soft black hair, moaning with each suck of his mouth. How was he so good at everything he did? I would never admit that to him, but I imagined I could come from him playing with my nipples.

Wetness gathered between my legs as he played with my breasts. He switched his mouth between them and used his hand to toy with the other. Pleasure filled me with each move of his mouth and hand, and I already felt like bursting.

His free hand slid lower to between my legs, discovering my wet pussy. He growled against my breast as his hand pushed in between my pussy lips.

"So wet already," Aladdin growled. "Is this all for me, Azalea?"

Not answering him, I pushed his head down to my pussy. With a low chuckle, he let me, kissing each piece of exposed skin he encountered on his way.

"So eager for my mouth," he mumbled, pushing away the fabric that covered my pussy.

With a groan, he dove in between my legs when I was fully naked. One long lick between my pussy lips made me almost shoot off the floor.

"Delicious," Aladdin growled before diving in again.

I didn't have a response for him, nor did he want one from me. His focus was on my pussy, and making me come as quickly as possible. Pleasure filled me with each swipe of his tongue, ending at my clit. His tongue drew circles around my clit, making my pussy clench with pleasure.

Sounds left me that didn't sound like me, but they only spurred him on. It was as if his only goal was to make me come as fast as I could and I was getting there steadily with each lick and suck.

My body was trembling, and my pussy was clenching around emptiness. It wouldn't be long before I burst and gave him the satisfaction of making me come so quickly. But it didn't matter anymore. All that mattered to me was getting to that high with his mouth on me.

The intense pleasure I felt when he placed his mouth on my clit and sucked was so overwhelming that I shattered into a thousand pieces. His name fled my lips as my body trembled with my release. Waves of pleasure washed over me as his tongue kept doing magical things to my pussy.

After a moment, it became too much, and I gently pushed him away. With another lingering lick, he sat up, looking every inch the smug thief that he was. But he hadn't stolen an orgasm from me. I had given it willingly.

Aladdin leaned over, our lips a hair's breadth apart. "I like you calling out my name in pleasure, Azalea."

"Shut up," I said, pulling him closer to me.

His mouth met mine in a slow dance of seduction. His taste mixed with mine created a deliciously new flavor that would haunt my dreams. I was already getting addicted to this thief, but I had to protect my heart before it would get stolen by him.

Taking control of this situation might not protect what had already been stolen, but it would ensure it stayed with that. I grabbed his shoulders and locked my legs around his hips, getting him off balance, and I rolled us around until I was on top again. I didn't dwell on his amazing body or the smug smile he threw at me from below. Even on the ground, with tousled hair and lips wet from my arousal, he looked every inch the master thief of this city.

Before he could say more annoying things, I grabbed his cock through the fabric of his trousers. It was already hard and throbbing in my hand, and I needed him inside of me as much as I had needed to steal that crown, maybe even more. This wasn't about revenge anymore. This was about what I wanted and I wanted to be fucked by this thief.

His eyes shot hot with desire, consuming me in its path. Aladdin opened his mouth, but I quickly caught his words with a kiss. His tongue was hot against mine, licking my mouth and devouring me in the kiss. My hands made quick work of his pants, uncovering his cock. When I grabbed it without any barrier between us, he groaned in my mouth, deepening the kiss. I gave him a few strokes before I positioned my pussy above it.

I broke the kiss, looking into his eyes while I slowly sunk down on his cock. He was big, but I was wet enough to ease the way. We both groaned in pleasure as he entered me, his size pushing me to my limits. Pleasure sparked as more of him filled me. It felt like he went on forever. My legs were trembling as I sunk lower until finally he was all the way inside of me.

His hands grabbed my hips, lifting me up to let me fall down again. Pleasure filled me with each move of his cock inside of me. I helped him and soon I was bouncing on his lap, riding him hard.

The sounds he made were from desire and pleasure and not snarky comments. I liked him quiet like this while I rode him, and I loved looking at his face, seeing the lust and pleasure radiate from him. I circled my clit with my finger, rushing me to my climax faster, only needing that one little push. Pleasure consumed me, and when my orgasm took over, my legs gave out. My pussy clenched around his cock, earning me a strangled groan from him as waves of pleasure washed over me.

With a loud groan, Aladdin turned us both over, lying me on my back, and fucking me hard against the cold floor. My orgasm only prolonged with each thrust he made. His name was on my lips, and mine on his as we came together in pleasure. I could feel his cock throb inside of me, and after a few more thrusts, he came as well, filling me with his cum. My pussy clenched and fluttered around him, milking all of his release from him.

He slowly pulled out and fell to the ground beside me. We were both breathing hard, quivering with the last of our release. I sighed, enjoying the afterglow of the orgasm and the silence. But, of course, he needed to break the moment.

"Why do you need the crown?" Aladdin asked.

I shrugged, not wanting to look at him and pop the little bubble I was in. For a moment, I had forgotten about the crown, the castle, and Jafar.

"Why do you need it?"

"Jafar has my friend," he said.

I turned my attention to him, and the truth was evident in the depths of his eyes. Suddenly, my need for revenge seemed trivial and childish. Aladdin might be a thief, but he was one with a good heart.

"I'll help you get them back," I said, grabbing his hand, and squeezing it comforting.

Aladdin squeezed back, pulling me into his embrace. "I think I'll enjoy working with you," he murmured in my hair.

"I think I will too," I said, hiding my smile against his chest.

THE END

If you enjoyed this story and want to know what happened with Princess Jasmine check out: The Genie[1]

The Huntsman

What if the Huntsman helped Snow White defeat the Evil Queen?

Don't eat the apple.

The Huntsman words were still fresh in my mind as I encountered the old lady. When she offered me a delicious-looking red apple, I accepted it with a smile.

Whatever you do, do not eat the apple. The Huntsman had told me all about the evil plans of my stepmother and what that apple would do to me if I swallowed it.

"Go on, dear. Take a bite," the old woman said, her voice rough with age, but all too familiar.

The spell she cast on herself was truly magnificent. Before me stood an innocent-looking old woman, clutching her basket full of apples with trembling hands. But her eyes and voice gave her away. If the Huntsman hadn't warned me, I would have believed the old woman. Her appearance was so sweet and innocent, playing into my weakness to trust too easily. I just hoped I hadn't put my trust in the wrong person.

"It looks delicious," I said with a smile as I lifted it up to my mouth.

My teeth pierced the red skin of the apple, the amazing taste filling my mouth, and for a moment I hoped that the Huntsman had been wrong. The sweet juice immediately turned bitter when I saw the evil glow in the eyes of my stepmother. I could feel the curse course through me, taking hold of my body, and I let it. My eyes closed, the apple fell out of my hand, and my body touched the ground.

I could hear the evil laugh of my stepmother above me echoing through the woods. She celebrated her win while I lay dying on the cold forest floor. Every ounce of compassion I ever felt for that woman burned away in that moment.

The evil queen was so confident in her curse that she didn't even check on me to confirm my death before leaving in her carriage. As soon as the stamping of the horses died down, the Huntsman ran to me. He pried open my mouth and pulled out the piece of the apple lodged in my throat. The curse slipped from my body and I could move my muscles again.

I immediately turned over and heaved out any remnant of the curse from my body. The Huntsman's comforting presence was next to me, offering me a drink to rinse my mouth.

"Thank you," I said.

I swished the water around in my mouth, making sure that I spit out every last taste of that rotten apple. I could still feel the curse in my body, but it was fading quickly now that the offending piece was no longer inside of me. The Huntsman offered me his hand to get up from the ground. I accepted it with a smile, swaying on my legs. Her magic still had some effect on me, but it would soon fade away. He steadied me with his firm hands on my hips, making a shiver of delight pass through me.

"It's my pleasure," he said.

"Thank you for being trustworthy," I said looking into his gorgeous gray eyes.

I had put my trust in so many people, but having been betrayed too many times to count, it became harder each and every time. I wasn't sure how much more my heart could take. But knowing that I could trust the man before me made the ache lessen just a bit.

The Huntsman cupped my cheek, and smiled, softening his sharp features. "You can always trust me, Princess."

His calloused hand felt rough against my soft skin, but I didn't want to lose his touch. I put my hand against him to keep it close to my face.

His eyes were on my ruby-red lips, and I couldn't resist the urge to lick them. A low growl came from him as he watched my tongue wet my lips. His thumb caressed my lower lip, his eyes fixated on the movement. I held my breath, hoping he would kiss me.

I wished he would lose control just once, so I could feel his lips on mine, but he was too honorable to do such a thing. I was promised to a prince from a faraway land, but everything I wanted was standing right in front of me.

Before I could ask him to take me, and let me forget all of my sorrows, he averted his gaze, and pulled his hand back. I sighed at the loss, my heart aching for so much more than one touch from him. But I knew that was the only time we had for now. I had a throne to conquer, and an evil queen to defeat.

The Huntsman and the dwarves had gathered an army that would fight in my name. Now that we had proof of the evil plans of the queen and the illicit way she had gained her throne, we could finally defeat her. My heart ached for the loss of my father, and the many years that had passed before I was able to fight back. I strengthened my resolve and pushed away any compassion I had for the woman who was once like a mother to me.

I led my army to battle, and we won. In a matter of days, I regained my rightful place on the throne, and the queen fled my land. I had my throne, my crown, and my land back. I had everything I wanted, but still, my heart ached, remembering that touch in the woods.

Sitting on my throne, my mind went back to my time with the dwarves. How I wished I wasn't a queen, and I could just go to the forest and be free, but I had a duty to my people that I couldn't ignore.

The door creaked open; the sound echoing through my throne room. My head lifted up, and as soon as my eyes met his, my heart started beating faster. Had he come for me? The Huntsman stepped forward, bowing on the steps in front of my throne.

"My queen. I have come to ask you to relieve me of my duties," he said his gaze firmly planted on my feet.

With those words, my heart shriveled. He wanted to leave me here all alone.

"Why?" I asked, my voice faint in the vast room, fit for a queen, even though I felt like a heartbroken girl.

After a moment of silence, he answered. "For personal reasons."

"Look at me when you address your queen!" I screamed, anger coursing through me. His eyes shot up and met mine. I could see so many emotions swim in them, reflecting the inner turmoil that was raging through me as well. "Why?" I asked again, my voice breaking.

In two steps he was standing in front of me, his head bowed so his eyes were level with mine. His hands were balled into fists at his sides as if he had to hold himself back from grabbing me.

"Because I cannot watch you marry another man," the Huntsman bit out, his warm breath fanning my face.

His confession made something bloom inside of me. "Then don't," I said. Confusion crossed his face as I grabbed one of his hands and put it on my cheek. I reveled in the feel of his calloused hands against my soft skin, aching for his touch. "Don't let another man marry me," I said. "Ask, and I will accept."

"Me?" he asked in wonder as his thumb caressed my cheek. "You'll marry a lowly Huntsman instead of a prince?"

"No," I said, shaking my head, grabbing his hand before he could pull it back. "I would marry you. A wonderful, brave man who stood by my side in battle instead of a man I've never even met."

"I don't know what to say. You're too generous, my queen. I could never be the man you need by your side."

"Would you love and protect me as you have done for so many years already?" I asked.

"Yes, of course, but..."

"That is all that I ask of you. Please. All I want is someone that loves me for me, and not for my title, my crown, or alliances between countries."

He nodded and kneeled before me, gently holding my hand. "Will you do me the honor of becoming my wife, Snow White?"

I jumped in his arms, tumbling us both over, but he grabbed me and kept me steady before I fell down the steps. "Yes, yes, a thousand times, yes!"

His lips met mine in a fiery kiss filled with passion, exactly how I imagined my first kiss to be. His mouth was rough underneath my soft one, and his earthy taste filled my senses. I moaned into the kiss, and his tongue slid between my lips, discovering more of my mouth, and deepening the kiss. The kiss went on forever, our hands never leaving each other, and our lips fused together with a desperation that took my breath away. I could feel his hardness against my stomach and I knew what needed to be done to make sure we could be forever together. I broke off the kiss to take in some much-needed air, but I never let go of him.

"Take me. Ruin me for any other man in the world, and make me yours," I said.

The wedding was planned to happen in two days, so I needed him to take my purity so I couldn't marry the prince. I was already plotting to rearrange the wedding so it would be an intimate ceremony between us.

"I've been yours from the moment I first saw you in the woods," my Huntsman said.

That moment felt like a lifetime ago when I had first fled the castle because my stepmother had tried to kill me. So much had happened since then, but my feelings for him had remained the same. He was the first man to show me compassion, and not be under the spell the evil queen seemed to be able to cast on men.

"And I yours. But I need you to take me as only a husband would take his wife so there is no doubt about it that I am yours, forever."

He growled against my lips, tightening his grip on me. "You test my patience, Snow White. I want to take my time, and show you all the pleasures that a union has to offer."

"We will have all the time in the world for that, but I need you now." I licked my lips and looked into his lust-filled eyes. "I need you to fuck me."

His eyes darkened with desire, and he made a hungry sound in the back of his throat. His hands ripped my dress open, exposing my breasts to the cool air. I gasped when his mouth descended on my breasts. Pleasure rushed through me as he covered my soft skin in kisses. His massive hands circled them, pushing them up so he could feast on them. My nipples hardened and ached for his mouth. I buried my hands in his hair to have something to hold on to as he showed me the pleasures of the flesh.

"So soft, pale, and perfect," my Huntsman groaned against my skin.

His hot mouth covered my nipple, and when he sucked on it I made a low throaty sound of pleasure. Sensations I've never experienced before rushed through my body and I didn't know what to do. It felt so good to have his mouth on me, exploring every piece of skin he encountered with his lips. I could feel pleasure course through me, and nestle low in my belly. Wetness gathered between my legs, and I squeezed them together to try and relieve the ache that was building there. When my nipple was hard and throbbing, he let it go with a pop.

"Beautiful red, against your white skin," he said before he went for the other one.

His lips, tongue, and even his teeth pleasured my breasts, and nipples until I was a moaning mess. Pleasure flooded my senses, but somehow I knew that I needed more.

"Please," I said, not sure what I was begging for, but he knew.

He let my breasts go, ripping the rest of my dress open. I didn't care that my royal gown was worth more than one of the dwarves' diamonds. All I cared about was getting naked, and letting him pleasure the rest of me. I tugged on his clothes, wanting to feel his skin against mine. My Huntsman swiftly undressed, and I made a happy little sound when I could let my hands rove over his body. He was all muscles, hard angles, and deliciously hairy. His magnificent cock rose from between his muscular legs, and I couldn't imagine taking something so big, and hard inside of my body.

"Don't worry, my queen," he said when he saw my wide eyes sizing up his cock. "I'll make sure you're ready for me."

He pushed my legs open, exposing my wet pussy to the cool air. His hungry gaze roved over my body.

"Gorgeous," my Huntsman growled before he dove down in between my legs.

All the air left my lungs when his mouth made contact with my pussy. Pleasure sparked with the first sweep of his tongue between my pussy lips, and sounds left me that I'd never produced before.

"Delicious," he said as he devoured me.

I couldn't reply as pleasure washed over me. My mind scrambled with everything he was doing to my body, but I knew I never wanted him to stop. His tongue focused on my pleasure spot, making stars explode underneath my eyelids. I hadn't even realized I had closed them, but it was as if he had more control over my body than I did.

His hands joined his mouth, opening my pussy lips for him to please me even better. He pushed at my entrance with an exploring finger, penetrating me for the first time. I gasped as I was so tight and even only one of his fingers was big. My pussy clenched around him, making my Huntsman groan. He slowly made me get used to his finger before he entered another. I felt so full, but I knew that I needed to be stretched more before I could take all of him.

With two fingers inside of me, he focused on my clit more. Circling it with his tongue, until pleasure rose inside of me, ready to burst. I made sounds of desire and pleasure as I could feel it rise steadily inside of me. When his mouth covered my clit, and he sucked, I exploded. My orgasm washed over me as waves of pleasure consumed me. My body trembled, my toes curled, and my pussy clenched around his two fingers. I screamed out in pleasure until my voice was hoarse.

My Huntsman made me come down from my amazing high with gentle touches. I opened my eyes to see the man that I would spend the rest of my life with gazing down on me with love in his eyes.

"I love you," I said, needing those words to be spoken out loud.

"I love you too," he said, leaning over to kiss me.

I could taste myself on his lips, mixed with his earthy taste that I had already grown to love.

"Please make me fully yours now," I said, pulling him on top of me.

We would have all our lives to discover and pleasure each other, but now I needed him inside of me. I opened my legs so he could kneel in between them, his massive cock looming over me. He had prepped me, but I still wasn't sure if it would fit.

"I'll go slow," he said reassuring me without me having to ask.

My Huntsman positioned his cock at my entrance, the tip hot against my pussy. Slowly he pushed inside of me, stretching me more than I thought I was capable of. I gasped as the invading thickness filled me. Inch after inch he gave me his cock. Every moment he checked in on me to see if I was in any pain.

"More," I moaned, knowing he was holding back and there was still so much more of him to fill me.

He growled low, pushing in further. Although it felt slightly uncomfortable, I was wet enough for him to ease the way. It felt like he went on forever, until finally he filled me up completely, bottoming out.

"Are you okay?" he asked with a pained expression on his face. "You're so tight."

"Yes, please move," I said.

My Huntsman eased out of me, then slid back in slowly, sparking pleasure deep inside of me. A surprised moan came from me as the tightness grew more comfortable, and pleasure filled me. He pulled out again, pushing back in with more force, and moans of pleasure tumbled from my lips. Encouraged by my sounds, his moves grew faster, and even more pleasurable.

"Faster, harder," I moaned, wanting him to lose control and fuck me without abandon.

He growled low, gripping my hips tighter, angling me in a way that each thrust pushed at a pleasure spot deep inside of me. In moments, my Huntsman was fucking me like a husband should fuck his wife, with lust and desire and without any restraint.

Every move sparked pleasure inside of me, growing bigger until it became too much. Pleasure washed over me as my climax took over my body. My pussy clenched around his cock, earning me a strangled groan. As he increased his pace, my orgasm surged through me. My body trembled, as my heart was beating a thousand miles a minute, flooded with so much love for my Huntsman. After a few more thrusts, I could feel his cock throb inside of me as his body shuddered. He released his seed, flooding my pussy and marking me as his. No one would be able to break our bond now.

"I love you so much, Snow White," he said while pushing away a strand of my sweaty, black hair. "I can't imagine a life without you."

"You will never have to. You have my heart, now, and forever, my love," I said.

Our mouths met in another passionate kiss as our bodies were still connected in the most intimate ways. We would deal with the formalities of our union later. For now, I just wanted to enjoy our pleasure together.

My Huntsman had saved me in more ways than one. He had showed me love again, healing my heart slowly.

THE END

The Bear

What if Goldilocks fell asleep in a single man's bed?

Fire surrounded me. I couldn't breathe, I couldn't think, all I could do was run. I ran until my legs couldn't carry me anymore and then I kept going, stumbling through the forest to safety. When I saw a cute house in the middle of a clearing, I almost cried with relief.

I knocked on the door, but all I heard was the echo of my own knuckles against the wood. As I grasped the handle, I was surprised to discover it was unlocked.

"Anyone here?" I called out as I slowly opened the weathered wooden door.

With a creak, it swung open into a cozy living area with a big couch and a table with three massive chairs. Whoever lived here was huge. I stepped inside, my legs trembling with fatigue. There were three different colored doors, red, yellow, and blue.

I just picked the first one, hoping for a bed. Behind the door, a massive bed greeted me and, without thinking, I let myself fall down on the soft sheets.

I would just close my eyes for a moment. Only for a moment.

"Who are you?!" an angry voice bellowed, waking me from my slumber.

I jumped up, looking at the terrifying face of a massive man looming over the bed. Bjorn Beren stood in front of me and I suddenly realized where his family got their name from. He looked almost exactly like a wild bear, massive and frightening, with a big black beard covering his face and piercing dark eyes that looked at me with disdain. Behind him, I could see an elderly couple that must be his parents.

"You still live with your parents?" I asked, my mouth working before my brain could kick into self-preservation mode.

He growled low; the vibrations creating a shiver across my back. "They live with me. They lost their house in the previous forest fire, and they are staying here until the repairs are done."

Fire. My house. It was all gone. A sob climbed up my throat and broke free before I could hold it back. Pushing past him, the elderly woman took a seat on the bed next to me, her gentle presence filling the room.

"Are you okay, dear? Did you run from the fire?" she asked.

I nodded, not able to speak without tears falling freely. "Come now, dear. I'll make you something to eat. You can stay here as long as you like," she said as she put an arm around me.

Her son opened his mouth, but after one pointed look from her, closed it again. He crossed his arms and stepped aside so she could lead me to the living area.

"Do you like porridge, dear?" she asked.

I nodded, hugging myself, shivering from the sudden realization that I had lost everything. All I had left in the world was the tattered gown I was wearing, its edges singed from the fire that had licked it. She threw a heavy blanket over my shoulders and directed me to sit on one of the massive chairs.

"That's my chair," Bjorn muttered.

"Well, she can't sit on the floor now, can she?"

"I have a kitchen stool out back," he said and left.

She turned back to me with a warm smile on her face. "How do you like your porridge? Hot, cold, or somewhere in between."

"Somewhere in between, I guess," I said and grabbed her hand before she could turn around. "Thank you for your kindness."

She patted it with a smile. "I understand how it feels to lose everything. But it will be alright. You came to the right house for help."

"What's your name?" I asked.

I had heard tales about Bjorn Beren, the woodworker from the forest, but I didn't know his parents.

"I am Ursa, my son is Bjorn, and my husband is Bjorn Senior," she said, pointing to the older man who hadn't said a word yet. He just sat on the couch reading the paper. "What's your name, dear?"

"Gilda," I said with a soft smile. "But everyone calls me Goldilocks because of my hair."

"You do have lovely hair, just a tad dirty at the moment. Why don't you clean up while I make the porridge?" she said, pointing at the blue door.

I entered the bathroom, gasping when I saw my reflection. Soot covered my entire body, and my typically blond hair was now a shade closer to brown. I cleaned up as best as I could, feeling slightly better already.

When I came back to the living area, they were all seated around the table, steaming bowls of porridge on the surface. Bjorn had placed a small stool between him and his mother. With a grateful nod, I took my place. I felt even smaller sitting between them on the low stool. They were really massive, but the gentle words of his mother had calmed me.

"Enjoy your porridge, Gilda," Ursa said.

I took a bite and almost moaned with delight. It was the perfect temperature between hot and cold, and she had added pieces of apple and a dash of cinnamon that elevated the taste to something excellent.

"It's perfect, thank you," I said when I swallowed my first bite.

"Thank you, dear. I am glad you enjoy the temperature. This one likes it scalding hot," she said, pointing to her husband. "And this one only eats it cold," she said with a nod to her son.

"Cold porridge?" I asked.

"Overnight oats," Bjorn muttered. "If you leave it soaking for a night, it will be soft and you can eat it faster."

When we all finished our porridge, Ursa ushered us to bed. "It has been a tiring day for everyone. So I think we shall all turn in."

Bjorn handed me a pillow and a blanket and nodded to the couch. "You can stay here for the night. Tomorrow we'll go into town to look for help."

"Thank you," I said, accepting the items. "I'm sorry for breaking into your house and sleeping in your bed."

"Don't mention it."

"Good night," I said, and he muttered in reply, already turning away to enter his bedroom.

As I lay on the couch, I could feel myself sinking into the plush, cushiony filling. I had never encountered such a soft couch before. No matter how much I twisted and turned, I couldn't find a comfortable position on the marshmallow-like surface. Eventually, I tried lying on the floor, wrapped in my blanket like a burrito, but the wooden floor was too hard for my back.

Bjorn's mattress had been a dream to sleep on. It had the ideal texture, not too hard, not too soft, and with just the right amount of springiness. I had fallen asleep in seconds, lying in his bed.

After a few hours of tossing and turning, I finally gave up. I quietly got out of bed and crept towards Bjorn's bedroom door. After a deep and steadying breath, I knocked on his door. No reply came, so I slowly turned the doorknob and eased the door open.

"Can I please join you?" I asked.

A rumbled response came that didn't sound like a refusal, so I tiptoed inside. "I'm really sorry, but the couch is too soft, and the floor is too hard."

Without a word, he pulled the covers back, allowing me to slide into the warmth. He felt like a massive hairy heater, and I just wanted to snuggle close to him. His weight on the mattress caused it to dip, and I found myself sliding towards his comforting, muscular arm.

"I'm sorry. I..."

"Stop apologizing, Gilda. If it wasn't okay, I wouldn't have let you," Bjorn rumbled low.

"Yes, of course. I'm..." I held onto the last word before it spilled from my lips and closed my eyes.

In no time I was asleep, enveloped in Bjorn's warmth and earthy scent. But fire followed me in my dreams. It didn't matter where I went. Flames were always licking at my heels. I tried to run as fast as I could, but the raging fire was always right behind me.

"Gilda, you're safe here." Bjorn's voice pulled me out of my nightmare and with a start, I sat up, shivering from the nightmare.

His arms came around me, comforting me in a way I didn't realize I needed. His touch grounded me and made me feel safe and secure in a place where the flames couldn't get to me. I clung to his arms until the tremors faded away.

"Thank you," I said, turning to look at his face, afraid to see pity.

All I could see in his eyes was understanding and compassion. Without another thought, I leaned over, touching his lips with mine.

When he didn't react, I pulled back and squeaked. "I'm sorry. I didn't-"

"Stop apologizing," Bjorn growled and kissed me back.

I melted into the kiss, letting him take the reins and just enjoying the experience. He tasted like cinnamon and dark chocolate mixed together. I moaned into his mouth, and he immediately took advantage of the opening to let his tongue play with mine.

Bjorn pulled me closer to him and I could feel his hardness against my stomach. Arousal coursed through me as my heartbeat sped up. I wanted him. I needed to feel him. Breaking the kiss, I gasped for breath, letting my hand wander lower until I gripped his erection.

Bjorn groaned, closing his eyes with pleasure.

"Can... Can I?" I asked, squeezing his cock.

His hand covered mine as he opened his eyes. "You don't have to do this, Gilda. I don't want you to feel pressured into anything."

I shook my head and I could feel him throb in my grip. "I really, really want to taste you, please."

Bjorn groaned and closed his eyes again. "No man in his right mind could ever refuse an offer like yours."

A chuckle escaped me as I slid lower. My hands traveled over his hairy chest, loving the feel of his coiled curls under my touch. I wanted to take my time exploring him, but his straining erection called to me. I grabbed him with both my hands and loved the groan that came from him.

This massive man was trembling underneath my touch, and I wanted him to lose control. I could barely contain his massive girth in my hands as I discovered his length. His cock was gorgeous, with throbbing veins running along its length, begging me to touch him.

A drop of precum pearled on the tip and I couldn't stop my urge from tasting him. I flicked out my tongue, licking up the drop, moaning when his taste exploded in my mouth.

I needed more. Caressing his length, I took the tip in my mouth and sucked. A low rumble sounded from him that I could feel vibrating through me all the way to my pussy. Wetness seeped out and arousal coursed through me as I sucked on his cock. His hand came to my head, pushing me down further until half of his length was in my mouth. He was too big. I couldn't fit everything in, but I tried.

I gagged and drooled, trying to fit more of his length in my mouth as Bjorn moaned with pleasure. The hoarse sounds coming from him only spurred me on. My hands caressed the part of him I couldn't suck, coaxing more of his pleasure from him. His cock throbbed underneath my hands, ready to burst at any given moment. I increased the pressure of my grip, sucking harder at the same time until he was continuously moaning with pleasure.

His whole body trembled, his cock throbbed and with a hoarse cry, he came. Bjorn filled my mouth with his seed, and I gulped it down, gently coaxing out the last of his release. The hand in my hair released its grip as he let himself fall back onto the mattress.

I crawled back up, licking my lips, swallowing down the last of his seed. Arousal was pulsing through me, but I was happy to go back to sleep, having pleasured him.

Bjorn rolled us around, trapping me under his massive body. "Let me return the favor," he growled in my ear, a shiver crossing through my body.

"You don't have to."

"I want to," Bjorn said, cupping my pussy.

I moaned and my eyes fluttered close. "O... Okay."

"Eyes open, gorgeous. I want you to look at me while I make you come," Bjorn growled.

My eyes shot open as he pushed a finger between my pussy lips. I moaned as I tried to keep my eyes focused on him, loving the lust and desire that burned in them.

"So wet and ready for me," Bjorn said as he circled my clit.

"Yes, please," I moaned, grabbing his powerful arm to keep me grounded.

Bjorn pushed one meaty finger inside, making my pussy clench around him. His hands were so big that it already felt amazing having only one finger inside of me. He slowly thrust in and out, making me get used to his size. I moaned low, needing more from him. He added another finger, scissoring them as he circled my clit with his thumb.

The pleasure was rising steadily with each move of his fingers. His eyes took in every change in my expression, noting which movements were the most pleasurable for me and repeating those.

"I'm so close," I moaned.

"I know. I can feel your pussy squeeze my fingers. Come for me, gorgeous," Bjorn growled low, increasing his movements.

My pussy fluttered around his fingers as pleasure rose. He circled my clit, increasing the pressure until I burst. A low, throaty sound of pleasure tore from my throat as my climax ripped through me. My pussy clenched around his fingers as pleasure filled my senses. My body trembled as my hand tightened around his arm. His eyes shone with satisfaction as he watched my orgasm wash over me.

"Beautiful," he murmured as the last of the tremors left my body boneless with pleasure.

Bjorn pulled his fingers out, raising them to his mouth. He licked them off, one by one, slowly, as if to savor my taste.

"Sweeter than the sweetest honey," he growled.

I could feel his cock harden again against my stomach. My pussy was greedy and needed more. I wanted to feel his big cock stretch like his fingers had done.

"Please, fuck me," I moaned.

"With pleasure," Bjorn growled, pushing my legs open.

He positioned his cock at my sopping wet entrance, slowly sinking in, making me moan with each inch he gave me. He stretched my pussy with his amazing girth, sparking pleasure deep inside of me.

"Please, move."

"Always so polite," Bjorn chuckled.

I gripped his hair and locked my legs around his hips, pulling him deeper inside of me. "Move, now."

"Whatever the lady wants," Bjorn growled, pulling back and thrusting back inside of me.

Sounds of pleasure I've never made before tore from my throat as he fucked me. My pussy fluttered around his massive cock every time he pulled back as if trying to keep him inside of me.

"So tight," Bjorn growled.

His chest hair rubbed over my nipples, making them pucker, only enhancing my pleasure. I loved his huge hairy body moving over my small one. His muscular arms framed my face, ensuring that his weight didn't overwhelm me. I felt cherished and safe in his embrace while he rocked my world with his massive cock.

Bjorn focused his eyes on my face as he pulled out and pushed back inside. Pleasure fluttered low above my pussy, and a moan tore from my throat. Each thrust only increased my pleasure, and his eyes locked on mine made me feel like I deserved that pleasure.

"Can you come like this?" Bjorn growled.

"M... maybe," I stuttered.

No one had ever asked me that question before. What he was doing was amazing, but I did need something more to come. Before I could assure him that this was good enough, he pulled out. A disappointed moan escaped me, but he stifled it with a kiss. His tongue danced with mine before he pulled back, and turned me over with his massive hands. Bjorn pushed a pillow underneath my hips and grabbed them to pull my ass back. In one move, he was back inside me, creating an amazingly new sensation.

"So deep," I moaned as I could feel him push into me further than before.

My pussy trembled around his cock, and Bjorn grunted. "Fuck yes, squeeze my cock."

I tightened my muscles and loved the groan that came from him. He pulled back and thrust back inside of me, hitting a spot I'd never felt before. My eyes squeezed shut as my pussy fluttered around him and pleasure shot through me.

"You feel amazing around my cock. Take your pleasure from me, Gilda. Play with your clit and come on my cock."

His words lit something on fire inside of me. I moaned as I pushed my hand underneath the pillow, finding my clit throbbing with pleasure. I circled it, sparking pleasure deep inside of me as he pulled back and pushed back inside of me.

"Yes, please, Bjorn," I moaned, not sure what I was begging for. All I knew was that I didn't want him to stop.

"Fuck, yes. I will never get enough of this pussy," Bjorn groaned as he fucked me harder.

Pleasure sparked with each thrust of his cock against that spot inside of me and every flick of my finger on my clit. The sensations became too much, and I came with a hoarse cry of pleasure. My body trembled as my pussy squeezed around him. Bjorn groaned low, fucking me through my orgasm, only enhancing my pleasure, murmuring sweet words in my ear.

"Come for me, gorgeous. Squeeze around my cock."

When the last tremor racked my body, he pulled out, turning me over again. My hips remained elevated on the pillow as he pulled me closer to him, entering me again. I moaned when his amazing cock stretched my sensitive pussy.

"Can I come inside of you?" Bjorn asked as he fucked me at a steady pace.

I nodded, squeezing my pussy around him with each thrust. My body was limp with pleasure and each thrust made me feel amazing. I wanted his cum. I wanted him to fill me up with his seed.

"Give me your cum," I moaned as I cupped my breasts.

His dark eyes shot hot with passion as he increased his pace.

"Fuck, you're gorgeous," Bjorn growled, grabbing my hips to pull me closer to him.

I could feel his massive body tremble as if trying to contain himself, but I wanted him to lose control. I squeezed my pussy around him, moaning how good he felt inside of me. Bjorn growled low, fucking me harder, and after a few more thrusts, he came. I could feel his cock throb inside of me as he filled me with his cum. His eyes squeezed shut as he climaxed and his contorted face was the most beautiful thing I had ever seen.

With a grunt, he pulled out and let himself fall next to me on the bed. He pulled me into his embrace, caressing my blond hair as I could feel his heart beat a thousand miles a minute.

"I want you to stay," Bjorn murmured in my hair.

I pushed up to look at his face and saw an earnest look in his eyes.

"You can stay as long as you want, and not just because that was the most amazing sex of my life. You don't have to feel obligated or anything, but-"

Before he could say another word, I kissed him. "I would love to stay," I said when I pulled back and snuggled closer to him.

Falling asleep in a stranger's bed might just be the best thing that ever happened to me.

THE END

The Mad Hatter

What if Alice returned to Wonderland as an adult?
Everyone expected me to marry a lord, but all I could think about was my time in Wonderland and the man I gave my heart to so many years ago. The Mad Hatter.

The only problem was that I'd never been able to find the entrance again. Since then, the passing years have left their mark on me, and I had almost resigned myself to giving up on my dream. However, everything changed on one enchanting spring evening.

I ran away from my suitors, not wanting to accept any offer of marriage just because I had a prominent family name. Maybe it was because I was desperate or maybe it was just fate, but suddenly I stumbled upon the entrance to Wonderland underneath the tree.

I recognized it in an instant and, without another thought, I jumped in. I fell longer than I could remember. It might have been a minute, a day, or a year. With a heavy thump, I landed in an octagon room filled with doors. Before I could figure out which one to open, one of them flew open with a bang and my Mad Hatter stood in front of me.

He looked exactly as I remembered him, dressed in flamboyant colors mismatched with his purple top hat, surrounded by a dark blue ribbon I had given him when we last met. His piercing dark green eyes and his too-big of a nose were like a breath of fresh air.

"Alice," he gasped as he opened his arms.

I jumped into his embrace, reveling in the feel of his powerful arms surrounding me.

"Have I gone mad?" he asked as he looked at my face in wonder.

"Only as mad as I have," I said with a laugh.

"Your hair," the Mad Hatter whispered, as he touched the red locks framing my face.

"I felt like I had outgrown the blond," I said, looking down, afraid to see the look on his face. "Do you like it?"

"I love it," he said, his voice filled with awe. "We match."

I looked up to see him touching his own hair, holding it next to mine, comparing the color. I nodded, feeling my throat ache from emotion.

"It was the only way to keep a piece of you with me when I was apart from you."

"Oh, how I have missed you, my Dear," the Mad Hatter said.

"And I you," I said, my voice hoarse with emotion.

It seemed like the years apart melted away as we looked into each other's eyes.

"Can I have that kiss now?" the Mad Hatter asked.

"I thought you'd never ask," I said with a smile.

Our mouths met in a kiss filled with the passion of years of longing. He tasted like all things great in life: laughter, joy, and passion. I moaned against his lips, laving it with my tongue, teasing him to open up. He granted me access and immediately let his tongue out to play. Our tongues danced as our teeth clashed in the whirlwind of our kiss.

Before the kiss could turn into something more, the Mad Hatter pulled back. He softened the move with a caress over my cheek with his thumb.

"But why did you return?" he asked. "It's not safe here. The Queen is still after you."

"There was nothing left for me in England. Everything I want is here with you. And I'm not scared of the Queen," I said.

My mother and sister had their own lives and only cared about getting me married off, so I wouldn't bother them with my crazy stories anymore. I didn't fit into the life of London. All I could think about was this world with my friends and the Mad Hatter.

"If you're not scared, neither am I," he said with a laugh.

"It is easy to be brave when I'm in your arms," I said.

"Then you should never leave."

"Never," I said and kissed him again.

The Mad Hatter kissed me back quickly but pulled back just as fast. "We should go before the Queen's guards find you."

"Lead the way," I said.

With my hand in his, he led me through Wonderland faster than I could have ever done on my own. He knew all the shortcuts and even had time to greet the people we met on the way without appearing to be rushed. I waved at the rabbit, cat, caterpillar, and all my other friends I had missed for so long, but we couldn't stay for a chat.

In no time at all, we arrived at his house. It was a wonderful, quirky building in the shape of a top hat that suited him perfectly. I could already imagine us living together in the small building, laughter filling every nook and cranny.

"Care for some tea?" he asked as we entered the house.

"I would love some, thank you."

The Mad Hatter made tea, catching me up on everything that had happened since I left Wonderland. I couldn't wait to visit my friends tomorrow, but tonight I only wanted him. When I finished my cup, I crawled on his lap.

"Are you sure about this, Alice?" he asked, caressing my hair. "I don't think I can give you my body as well as my heart, knowing you will leave me again."

"I won't leave you. Trust me. I'm here to stay with you forever. Your mind, body, and heart are safe with me," I said, cupping his cheek and caressing his lips.

"We're both mad here," he said with a smile.

"I'm afraid so. But you and I both know that only the best people are."

The Mad Hatter kissed me, and I sighed happily against his mouth. We were together in his house in Wonderland and I could finally be with someone who understood me. Our tongues touched, and I loved his taste filling me. I moved my hips until I was grinding against him, feeling his cock harden underneath me. He groaned into the kiss, his hands grabbing my hips, increasing the pressure on my clit.

Arousal coursed through me, and I was so ready for him to make me his forever. Our kiss turned heated as our hands discovered each other. I ripped his shirt open, scattering buttons on the floor, letting my hands roam over his naked skin. My hands wandered lower, gripping his growing erection through his pants.

The Mad Hatter let out a pained groan, throwing his head back and closing his eyes. His hat fell on the floor with a loud thunk.

"Fuck Alice. I've been dreaming of this for so long. Please tell me this isn't a dream."

"If it is, I never want to wake up," I said and kissed him again.

He grabbed my hair with his hand, angling my head so he could plunder my mouth. I moaned into the kiss as his tongue played with mine. His cock strained against his pants, begging to be released. I grabbed it through the fabric and with a groan, he broke the kiss.

"Please, Alice. I might burst if you continue. I want you too much. Let me make it good for you first," he begged.

I giggled as his words flowed through me like a strong brandy, making my insides warm.

"Or I could make you come in my mouth. That way you don't have to worry anymore," I said.

The Mad Hatter closed his eyes again with a groan. "Dear heavens, you have no idea what you do to me."

"Hmm, I think I do," I said, squeezing his rock-hard erection.

Before he could protest, I slid off his lap to the floor in between his legs. I opened his pants, releasing his cock and gasping at my first look at it. It was absolutely magnificent. His cock was enormous, hard, and throbbing for release. The head was leaking drops of precum that I immediately licked off. His salty taste exploded in my mouth, and I moaned with delight. The groans coming from above me only spurred me on.

I gripped his impressive length, marveling over his size. I could barely wrap my fingers around him, and I just knew he would feel delicious inside of me. My pussy fluttered achingly empty and arousal filled me. Throbbing veins covered his entire length, leading me down to his balls. I grabbed them in my hand, loving the strangled sounds that came from him. I wanted to take my time exploring him, but I also wanted to relieve some of his pressure.

As I looked up, I could see how hard he was trying to maintain control. His hands were balled against his sides, his head was arched upward, and I could see a vein throbbing in his neck. My poor Hatter looked even crazier now than before.

I didn't want to waste another second, so I bent over and took the head of his cock into my mouth. His taste and smell filled my senses, and arousal coursed through me. I used both of my hands to stroke his length up and down as I sucked hard.

His hips thrust upwards almost involuntarily, so I opened my mouth wider to take in more of his length. My hands moved over his length, trying to touch every inch of him. The Mad Hatter was speaking gibberish, only spurring me on more. I tightened my grip and increased my movements as I sucked in more of him.

"Fuck, Alice," he screamed, and that was all the warning I got before his seed filled my mouth.

I swallowed it down greedily as more spurts erupted from his cock. With gentle movements I coaxed out his release, loving the way he had exploded under my touch. As I sucked out the last of his release, I could feel him trembling and his cock twitching in response. With a final lick of his tip, I pulled back, touching the edges of my mouth to ensure none of it had gone to waste.

The Mad Hatter sagged in his chair with a dazed look on his face. "I've never come so hard in my entire life," he said.

"And I never had quite such a lovely treat," I said with a wink.

I couldn't wait to do that again, and again for the rest of our lives together. My pussy was leaking with wetness and achingly empty as I climbed on his lap again. His hands immediately pushed my dress up, caressing my thighs.

"So soft, so pure, and all mine," the Mad Hatter murmured in awe as his hands traveled higher.

"Yes, all yours," I moaned when he reached my soaked panties.

"So wet, and ready for me," he said as his finger dipped under the fabric, grazing over my pussy.

A hum of satisfaction left me as he finally touched me where I was aching the most. His long and nimble fingers played over my pussy as if I was an instrument he needed to tune. Pleasure rose inside of me with every caress.

"I need to taste you," he said.

Before I could reply, he lifted me up in his arms, kicked his pants to the side, and ran up the stairs. Another giggle escaped me as I bounced in his arms and he almost missed a step in his enthusiasm. I just knew that our lives together would be like this, filled with love, lust, and laughter.

When we reached his bedroom, he dropped me on the bed and immediately dove in between my legs. My laughter turned into moans of pleasure as he ripped away my panties and devoured my pussy. I grabbed his red curls, urging him on.

His tongue slipped between my pussy lips, finding my clit and licking me to an inch from my life. Sounds I've never made before fell from my lips as pleasure rose inside of me. His hands gripped my legs tight, keeping them spread wide so he could access my pussy easily. The

Mad Hatter licked and flicked and sucked and made me feel like I was the best treat in the world that he couldn't get enough of.

"Please, yes, more", I moaned incoherent words, trying to spur him on without knowing what I was saying.

Even though I wasn't making any sense, he understood what I needed. He pushed one long finger inside of my pussy, making me almost shoot off the bed. He held me steady as his tongue and finger worked together to give me more pleasure than I could ever imagine. When he added a second and third finger, my pussy clenched around him as if trying to keep him inside.

"Delicious, tight, wet," he groaned against my pussy as he moved his fingers at a steady pace.

I was strung tight, ready to burst, when he arched his fingers upwards, touching a spot deep inside of me that made me see stars. With a pleasured cry, the release that had been building up inside of me washed over me. My body trembled as my pussy squeezed around his fingers. The Mad Hatter sucked on my clit, only prolonging my pleasure as he kept caressing that spot inside of me. I moaned, gasped, and writhed under his touch as waves of pleasure washed over me, consuming me.

When my pussy became too sensitive with the overload of pleasure he gave me, I pushed him away. After one last lingering lick, he pulled back. He sucked off his fingers, glistening with my juices, moaning in pleasure.

He looked absolutely mad. His hair stood upright facing every which way, his red lips were plump from sucking me and his eyes glittered with lust. His cock had hardened again during his feast on my pussy, and I needed him inside of me.

"Take me, please," I moaned.

"So deliciously polite, Alice," the Mad Hatter laughed. "There still is some London inside of you, my Dear."

I grabbed his cock, pulling him to me, changing his laugh into a moan. "Fuck me, now," I growled.

His eyes shot hot with lust as he positioned his cock at my entrance. "With pleasure," he said as he pushed into me.

Words left me as his cock stretched my pussy in the best way. Inch after delicious inch filled me, and it felt like he went on forever.

"Fuck, you're tight," the Mad Hatter growled as he pulled back and pushed back in, giving me even more of his length.

My pussy fluttered around him as if trying to pull him in even deeper.

"That's because you're so big," I moaned.

He pushed in the last inch of his cock, filling me to the brink.

"Perfect fit," he said before he pulled back and thrust back inside of me, sparking pleasure with each move.

"Yes, we were made for each other," I said as I grabbed his shoulders to have something to hold on to as he rocked my world.

"Play with your clit," the Mad Hatter said while he grabbed my legs and pulled them higher. "I want you to come around my cock."

"Oh, yes," I moaned, pushing my hand in between our bodies, circling my clit with my finger.

Pleasure sparked as he fucked me hard. I loved the look on his face as my pussy clenched around him. His hair swished wildly around his face and his eyes were burning bright with lust and love. My pussy was still sensitive from my first orgasm and soon I could feel another rise steadily inside of me. With each thrust, it became bigger and bigger. My finger circled around my clit faster, chasing that high again, wanting to come with his cock deep inside of me.

"So beautiful. Come for me, Alice," the Mad Hatter said.

His words ignited my orgasm and I could feel it flow through my body. Pleasure washed over me as my pussy squeezed around his cock. He growled and increased his pace, fucking me hard and fast.

A scream of pleasure tore from my lips as my climax ripped through me. My back arched from the bed as my toes curled with pleasure. When the last tremors left my body, my head fell back with a sigh.

"Another," he growled as he fucked me harder, like a madman.

"I don't think I can come again," I moaned as I was riding a near-painful edge.

"The only way to achieve the impossible is to believe that it is possible," the Mad Hatter said with a wink.

I laughed as he threw my own words in my face, but he was right. Even though I didn't think I had another one in me, he proved me wrong in the best way. After a few more thrusts, pleasure washed over me again, and this time he followed me.

My pussy spasmed around his cock as my body trembled from my climax. I could feel his cock throb deep inside of me as he filled me with his seed. Pleasure sizzled through every part of me and filled my heart with love. My pussy milked out the last of his release as he let out a shuddering sigh.

"This couldn't possibly be a dream, because even my imagination couldn't come up with something this good," the Mad Hatter whispered.

Another laugh escaped me, making my pussy squeeze around him again. With a groan, he pulled out, giving my abused pussy a moment of relief.

"I promise that this isn't a dream, my love," I said as I cupped his cheek and pulled him down for a kiss. "I'm really here, and I am here to stay forever."

"Forever together sounds wonderful," the Mad Hatter said, letting his forehead rest against mine.

"It does," I said.

He rolled off me, pulling me into his embrace and I felt like I was whole again. I belonged in the arms of the man I loved, ready to face whatever evil would come for us together.

THE END

Bluebeard

TW: *thought of suicide, loss of a spouse because of suicide.*

What if the Little Mermaid found love with Bluebeard?

Trading my voice for a set of legs had seemed like a great idea at the time. But when I saw the man I had given my heart to kiss another woman, it all fell into ruins. I stood at the edge of a cliff overlooking the raging water. As a storm brewed on the horizon, my father's urgent calls beckoned me back home. I opened my mouth to scream, momentarily forgetting that my voice was gone. My throat ached and tears streamed down my face, but no sound came out of my mouth.

Just as I took a step forward, a hand grabbed mine, pulling me back to safety. I turned around and stared into the face of the ugliest man I had ever seen. A big blue beard covered the bottom half of his face. The strange color, close to the way the ocean water looked before a storm, looked hideous against his weathered face. His dark eyes were the only thing that elevated the look. They had a sadness that felt similar to my own. When I didn't make any move to throw myself off the cliff again, he dropped my hand.

"Are you alright?" he asked with a rough voice, matching his appearance.

I opened my mouth to answer, but only silence greeted my ears, so I shook my head.

"Can you speak?" he asked.

I shook my head again, grabbing my throat, and feeling the spell wrapped around it.

"Can I take you home?" he asked.

I turned around, looking at the ocean, the waves beckoning me closer. One more step and I would be home, but I couldn't face my father, knowing he had been right all along. Humans were not to be trusted.

The man took a step closer and I could feel his body heat against my back. I wanted to snuggle closer to him, have him wrap my arms around me, and tell me it would be alright, but he was a stranger.

"Do you have a home?" he asked.

I shook my head, my eyes on the waves. After a final, silent goodbye, I turned back to him.

"Please, come with me. I can give you some hot food and fresh clothes to give you time to figure out what you want to do."

A small smile grazed my lips, the first one since I turned into a human, and I nodded. He took me to his home not too far from the cliffs. It was a majestic building with a tall tower that looked over the surrounding land. He told me his name, Bluebeard, and that he always walked alongside the cliffs in the evening before bed. He was a captain who spent the winter in his home, waiting for the weather to turn so he could sail the seas again.

When we entered his house, I was greeted by a very sparsely decorated room. It had two chairs and a table, but not much more, even though there was so much space. Humans were odd in their own way. Some wanted every inch covered and others needed to have space to walk around in.

Bluebeard handed me two plates and some bent metal and directed me to go set the table. I recognized the dinglehopper, but I wasn't sure why he would want me to put it on the table. I stacked them up in the middle with the dinglehopper and pointy thing sticking out on both sides. Happy with my effort, I turned to him with a smile. He came back with a big pot of steaming soup that smelled delicious. My stomach growled in response, and I realized I had eaten nothing since coming to land.

Bluebeard put the pot on the table and sorted the plates and cutlery on either side in front of a chair. I felt stupid, realizing how wrong I had been, but he didn't admonish me in any way. He put some soup on both plates and pointed to the empty chair.

"Please, join me. I'm not the greatest cook, but I keep myself alive."

I sat on the chair, eying him to see what he would grab on how he would use it before I made a fool of myself again. He grabbed the utensil with the round edge, put soup in the hollow end, and lifted it up to his mouth. He blew on the soup before putting it in his mouth.

"If you are checking if I am going to die from the food, you might have to wait a while," Bluebeard said with a dry chuckle.

A half smile appeared on my face as I looked at my delicious-smelling plate. I could do this. I grabbed the same utensil he had and scooped up some liquid. Mimicking his movement, I blew on it, and put it in my mouth, surprised by how good it tasted. I wanted to thank him, but my voice wouldn't let me, so I raised the utensil at him with a smile and took another bite.

After the meal, Bluebeard showed me to a separate bedroom, and I fell asleep without a second thought. For the first time since turning into a human, I didn't feel alone.

I stayed with him, keeping him company as he showed me how to do the menial tasks around the house, as well as how it all was called. He didn't think less of me for not knowing how a broom worked or how to wash clothes. Bluebeard was a patient man who explained everything to me until I understood. The only thing that he didn't do was touch me. I didn't know why and it was hard to ask without my voice, but every time I reached out for his hand, he pulled back.

After a few weeks, he wanted to teach me how to write so we could communicate better. He taught me the entire Alphabet and his name, so I could finally show him mine. I didn't know how I knew how to write my name, but I did.

"Aril?" Bluebeard asked as he saw it written.

I shook my head and underlined the e after the I. "Ariel?"

I nodded, clapping my hands, happy that he finally knew my name.

"Hi Ariel, nice to meet you," Bluebeard said with a low chuckle.

I loved his laugh. It made his entire face less hideous and his eyes lost some of the sadness. I've wanted to ask about his grief, but I never know how to breach the subject. His ring glinted in the candlelight and I suddenly remembered something about the significance of it. There should be a second one that another person wore.

I touched the band on his hand, cocking my head and looking at him with a question in my eyes.

Bluebeard played with the ring, turning it round and round his finger as his eyes became sad again. "Are you asking about my wives?"

I nodded, wanting to know why he was all alone in his massive home. A weary sigh escaped him as he pulled off the ring.

"I suppose I should tell you. It is only fair," he said with a nod. "I was married a few times. I have a lot of money, so I was a suitable marriage candidate when I was young, but my wives didn't agree with me. They all killed themselves on our wedding night by jumping off the tower."

A gasp escaped my lips as I realized how it must have felt for him to see me ready to jump off those cliffs.

Bluebeard grabbed an old key from his chain, showing it to me. "That is why the tower is off limits, Ariel. There is only one key, and it will remain closed until the day I die. I don't want to lose anyone else like that ever again."

I nodded, fascinated by the way the light shone on the key. It was almost as if it was calling to me, begging me to use it and go to that room.

"Please, Ariel. You have to promise me you will never go to the tower," Bluebeard said, grabbing my hand.

I nodded again, realizing how much it meant to him. He had been so kind to me, and I would never betray his trust. I put my hand over his, enjoying the warmth that came from his skin, but he pulled it back. He had been careful not to touch me since I had entered his home, as if afraid of something. It was hard to understand his thoughts and feelings when I couldn't ask him about them.

We both went to bed as we did every night, but I couldn't sleep. That key kept occupying my thoughts. I had felt something when I saw it, and I needed to figure out what it meant.

Even though I didn't want to break my promise to Bluebeard, I couldn't stop myself from getting out of my bed and up those old stairs. The key was already in my hand, begging me to use it, even though I had no memory of grabbing it. The wind was howling outside and the whole tower seemed to sway with it. I had to hold myself steady against the cold stone walls to get up the creaking steps.

When I reached the door, the pull felt even stronger. As if there was some kind of magic floating around, pulling me in. I lifted the key with trembling hands and it got sucked into the lock. With a click, it turned, and the door swung open. Immediately powerful magic took hold of me and pulled me further into the room. I tried to fight it, grabbing the walls and the wooden door frame, but to no avail. My legs betrayed me and stepped over the threshold onto the wooden floor.

A scream tore from my throat as the magic from the tower fought with the spell that already had a hold of me. When that sound erupted from me, I immediately yelled out Bluebeard's name, hoping he would come in time to save me.

My legs walked over to the open window on the opposite side of the room on their own. I could see the Ocean calling me, trying to get to me, but there was too much land between us.

When I reached the edge of the window, my hands grabbed anything they could hold, the weathered wood scratching my palms. The land beneath me felt so far away. This was not how I wanted to go. I didn't want Bluebeard to think I had killed myself like his wives had. I didn't want the last thing that I would see before the end to be dirt instead of water. I wouldn't die this way.

I screamed again, my voice hoarse and far from the Siren song that I used to sing. My fingers tried to grab the weathered wood of the window, but I could feel it peal off, leaving my hands empty. One more step and gravity would pull me down, but a hand grabbed mine.

Bluebeard charged into the room just in time to grab me and pull me into the safety of his embrace. The magic fell flat, as if disappointed it hadn't been able to claim another victim.

I looked up at his weathered face and dark blue beard. It was hard to imagine I found him ugly only weeks ago, as I now saw the face of a brave man who had been nothing but kind to me. Bluebeard had saved my life, not once, but twice already.

"You saved me," I said, my voice a hoarse whisper, but he heard me.

I lay trembling in his arms as he cupped my cheek with a gentle touch. "I will always save you. As you have saved me from a lonely life as a widower."

"There was magic, a curse," I said as I put my hand against his, not wanting him to let go.

Bluebeard nodded with a sad look on his face. "I had suspected something, but I was never sure. My first wife was a sorceress and did not want to marry me."

When I wanted to say something else, my legs gave out, and I could feel the magic holding them together, leave me. With the curse from the tower, the hold that the sea witches' magic held on me faded, and my legs would soon turn back into a tail.

"What is it? How can I help?" Bluebeard asked with a worried look on his face.

"I need to tell you something," I said, my voice slowly regaining strength with each word. "I was a mermaid once, trading my voice for my legs. But now that I have my voice back, it seems that the magic from my legs will go back to the sea."

"How can we fix it?" Bluebeard asked, supporting me as he let himself slide against the wall.

"Only a true love kiss can-"

His mouth covered mine, breaking off the rest of my words. I moaned into the kiss, my first kiss, and I felt my legs regaining their strength.

"You love me?" I asked in wonder as he pulled back.

Bluebeard nodded, caressing my cheek. "And I suppose you love me too if this worked?"

"I do, so much," I said, kissing him again.

Bluebeard tasted like the sea and land mixed together, salty and musky and absolutely perfect. His tongue came out to play with mine, and I moaned into the kiss, never wanting it to end.

When we broke the kiss to catch some much-needed air, I didn't want to let him go. "Please make me yours," I said.

"Will you marry me?" Bluebeard asked.

"Yes, a thousand times, yes, but I want you now. I don't want to wait until our wedding night."

Bluebeard growled low in his throat and picked me up in his arms. Taking two steps at a time, he ran to his room, throwing me on the bed.

"I can't wait to have you, either. I have dreamed about this moment for so long. Of touching you, kissing you, discovering your body."

"Please do all of those things," I said as I let my dress slip from my shoulders.

I wanted to be naked underneath him and feel his touch on my skin. He moaned when I exposed my breasts to the cold air of his room. My nipples pebbled and goosebumps spread over my arms.

"You're cold. Let me make a fire," Bluebeard rumbled, turning towards the fireplace.

"No, I don't want to wait another moment. Warm me with your body. Please Bluebeard."

A shiver racked his form as he closed his eyes for a moment. "I won't be able to control myself, Ariel."

"I don't want your control. I want your passion, your love, your cock," I moaned as I pushed away the fabric from my dress and opened my legs, exposing my pussy.

I had been silent for too long, and now that I had my voice back, I would use it to get what I wanted. No more wasting time, no more longing for change. I needed him now. I was wet between my legs, ready for his cock, achingly empty.

I knew how to pleasure myself, but I hadn't experienced it with someone else before. I wanted him to be my first and last. Bluebeard looked at me with so much lust in his eyes, it took my breath away. He grasped his hard cock through his trousers, stroking it slowly as he looked at my naked body.

I beckoned him closer with my finger as I let my other hand slip in between my legs. A strangled groan came from him when I opened my pussy lips with my fingers, showing him how wet I was.

A shiver washed over me. I didn't know if it was from the cold or from the desire to have him, but it pushed him into action. Bluebeard kneeled on the bed in between my legs. With slow, unsure movements, he caressed my legs with his warm hands.

After not having been touched for so long, his rough hands felt amazing on my skin. I wanted more. I needed more of his touch, but I was afraid to scare him away with my demands. He seemed so unsure to touch me as if he had never done this before.

"Your skin is so soft and perfect," Bluebeard said in awe.

"Your hands feel so good and warm," I said.

"I don't feel good enough for you," Bluebeard said, and I could hear the heartache in his voice.

I sat up, scooting closer to him, and grabbed his hands in mine. "You are the best man in the whole world and I would be honored to become your wife. I never told you why I traded my voice for legs in the first place," I said, cupping his face, caressing his blue beard, and loving how soft it was underneath my touch. "I did it for a man I thought I loved, but I didn't know what love was. What I feel for you is real love, and I want to experience everything with you for the first and last time."

I kissed him, loving how his beard tickled my chin and naked breasts. He deepened the kiss, grabbing my head, and pulling me closer to him. His tongue played with mine, as I let my hands wander lower over his chest to his trousers. Bluebeard groaned when I grabbed his erection through the straining fabric, breaking the kiss.

"You don't mind my age or my blue beard?" he asked.

"I love your beard. The color reminds me of the Ocean, and I am a 150-year-old siren. Do you mind my age?" I asked.

"You are perfect," he said. "And all mine."

"Yes, now fuck me," I said, squeezing his cock.

"I need to taste you first," Bluebeard said, gently laying me down on the sheets.

"Taste me?" I asked.

"Yes, I want your arousal on my lips and in my beard so I can smell you for the rest of the night."

"Oh, okay," I said, my voice wavering as arousal coursed through me.

I opened my legs again, and he bent down in between them. His beard brushed the inside of my thighs as his mouth descended on my pussy. A moan came from me when his lips made contact with my heated skin. I was so wet and ready for him.

His tongue slipped between my pussy lips as his beard caressed the rest of my pussy and ass. Pleasure rose inside of me as his tongue discovered my pleasure points. Bluebeard licked deep into my pussy and then flicked up until he met my pleasure bud. I moaned when his tongue focused on my pleasure point, my pussy squeezing around nothing, achingly empty.

"I want you inside," I moaned.

Bluebeard immediately pushed a finger inside, my pussy squeezing around it greedily. His tongue drew circles around my pleasure bud as he slowly fucked me with his finger. Pleasure rose steadily inside of me, but I still wanted more. I wanted all of him.

"More," I moaned. "I want your cock."

"So greedy," Bluebeard rumbled against my pussy, causing vibrations to wash through me.

"I don't want to wait another second to have you inside of me. Please, Bluebeard."

"I will do everything that you ask of me, my love," Bluebeard said.

After a last, lingering lick, he lifted up from my pussy and opened his pants. For the first time, I got a look at the equipment he was packing and I was not disappointed. His hard cock sprung free from its confinement, as eager for it as me. I wrapped my hand around it, loving how his velvety warmth felt underneath my fingers. He was hard, but soft at the same time, like a rod wrapped in the softest velvet. I knew he would feel amazing inside of me, and I didn't want to wait for him anymore.

"Fuck me, make me yours, forever," I said.

Bluebeard groaned, and I could feel his cock throb under my touch. "I might not last for long. If I had known you had such a filthy mouth, I would have kissed you far sooner."

I laughed, the sound rough but melodious at the same time. I might never have my Siren song back, but all I really needed was here in front of me.

"Now you can kiss me anytime you want for the rest of our lives," I said.

Bluebeard kissed me, and I moaned when his taste mingled with my arousal. He positioned his cock at my entrance, and I groaned when he slowly pushed inside. I was wet enough, but it still stung a bit when he stretched me to take his girth. With a gasp, I broke the kiss so I could breathe through the pain. He was breathing heavily as he gave me inch after delicious inch of his cock.

"Are you okay?" Bluebeard asked as he saw my face.

"Yes, don't stop. I want all of it," I said, grabbing his hips to keep his cock inside of me.

With a strangled groan, Bluebeard pushed in the rest of the way, filling me with his amazing cock. I've never felt so full and complete in my life. It was as if he was the missing piece that I had been searching for, for so long.

I could feel his massive body tremble on top of me as if trying to maintain control. I wrapped my legs around his waist, pushing my hips up to get him to move. With a low rumble of pleasure, he pulled back and pushed inside of me. The pain dissipated and only pleasure remained. I made a low throaty sound of pleasure as he fucked me, sparking pleasure with every move.

I never wanted this feeling to end. Our connection was so pure and filled with lust and love that it almost felt magical.

"I love you," I moaned as pleasure flowed through me.

"I love you too," Bluebeard groaned as he fucked me harder.

Every thrust felt like coming home and feeling more at ease in my body. My legs were mine and without the curse wrapped around my throat, I could moan freely. My pussy fluttered around his cock with each backward pull, as if trying to keep him inside of me.

"So good, so tight, Ariel," Bluebeard groaned.

I could feel his cock throb deep inside of me, pleasure sparking with each thrust. I knew it wouldn't be long before pleasure would take over my body, but I wanted him to join me.

"More, harder, faster," I moaned as my pussy squeezed around his cock.

"By the Seas, Ariel. I don't think I can hold it much longer."

"Yes, give me your cum. Fill me with your seed," I moaned.

Bluebeard fucked me harder, sparking pleasure with each thrust as the sounds he made became louder. I loved hearing his cries of pleasure. I was so focused on him that I almost didn't realize my own climax was taking me by surprise. After another deep and hard thrust, the pleasure inside of me suddenly burst. I came with a pleasured cry as my pussy squeezed around him. Pleasure took over and my legs tightened around him, keeping him buried deep inside of me.

He groaned low as he came as well. His cock throbbed and spurts of seed filled me as my pussy milked all of his release from him. My body trembled as pleasure flowed through me, filling all of my senses. It was too much, too good, too perfect with him. It was almost as if I ceased to exist and all I could feel was his cock deep inside of me and pleasure filling my whole body.

Bluebeard slowly pulled out after he had filled me with all of his seed. He rolled over, pulling me with him into his arms. His embrace made me feel sated, happy, and safe.

"As soon as the weather breaks, I will start sailing again," he said. "I would love for you to join me, Ariel."

I looked up at him and saw the love and devotion I felt for him reflected in his eyes. "I would love that. You could meet my family."

He kissed me, pulling me close to him, and I sighed happily against his body. It might have been the best decision of my life to trade my Siren voice for legs.

THE END

Authors Note

Give it up for collection numero 3! I honestly thought I was going to write a few erotic fairytale retellings, but somehow I just keep writing more! I can't believe I already wrote 15 short stories and that this is my third bundle, but it is and I am so happy to share it with you!

This collection has some classics, but also some less known stories, I can never pick a favorite, because I truly loved writing every single one of them!

Did you know you can get a signed paperback in my Etsy Shop? I even have a matching bookmark and some fun stickers that you can get with it!

Anyway, I hope you enjoyed the collection! Please leave a rating and/or a review if you did.

About the author

Lilith Leana writes what she loves; Monster, fantasy, and sci-fi erotica.

Born and raised in Belgium, she devours ebooks as if it heals her. In her day job she loves to organize, plan and make schedules for other people, but when the night falls she can let loose with her fantasies which star all kinds of Monsters and Human couplings.

YOU CAN ALSO FIND ME on:

New Author Website: https://lilithleana.wordpress.com/

New Newsletter! Sign Up to be kept up to date about my new releases, sales, character art, and giveaways: Sign Up Form[1]

Instagram: https://www.instagram.com/lilithleana/

Etsy Shop: https://www.etsy.com/be/shop/SteamyPublishing

Or you can email me: lilith.leana666@gmail.com

DEAR READER

If you enjoyed this book, please consider leaving a review. Indie writers depend on reviews to keep writing and publishing.

Thank you so much ❤

Lilith

---

1. https://dashboard.mailerlite.com/forms/533589/95138330138642151/share

Also by the author

Series & Collections

[Creature Loving Volume 1: A Monster Erotica Collection](1)
[Creature Loving Volume 2: A Monster Erotica Collection](2)
[Creature Loving Volume 3: A Monster Erotica Collection](3)
[Creature Loving Volume 4: A Monster Erotica Collection](4)
[Creature Loving Volume 5: A Monster Erotica Collection](5)
[Creature Loving Holidays 1: A Monster Erotica Collection](6)
[Grim Lovers 1: An Erotic Fairytale Collection](7)
[Grim Lovers 2: An Erotic Fairytale Collection](8)
[My Ghostly Lover](9)
[My Orc Mate](10)

Fairytale Retelling Short Stories

[The Beast](11)

---

1. https://books2read.com/u/47gLkj

2. https://books2read.com/u/47VMwA

3. https://books2read.com/u/bW0pk1

4. https://books2read.com/u/3LxQD1

5. https://books2read.com/u/4AaD90

6. https://books2read.com/u/bp6Yyg

7. https://books2read.com/u/4AA7Zp

8. https://books2read.com/u/mZpjNe

9. https://books2read.com/u/3J6dxJ

10. https://books2read.com/u/3yd90L

Hook[12]

Frost[13]

The Jungle Man[14]

Rumpelstiltskin[15]

The Frog Prince[16]

The Genie[17]

Peter & Pan[18]

The Fae Guardian[19]

The Dragon[20]

The Thief[21]

The Huntsman[22]

The Bear[23]

The Mad Hatter

11. https://books2read.com/u/4ENaEA

12. https://books2read.com/u/4Nolg9

13. https://books2read.com/u/mvyGrX

14. https://books2read.com/u/3R0Aqj

15. https://books2read.com/u/bryN0w

16. https://books2read.com/u/bMzzY8

17. https://books2read.com/u/brexek

18. https://books2read.com/u/4AAqkp

19. https://books2read.com/u/38n6K6

20. https://books2read.com/u/br6YAW

21. https://books2read.com/u/mKXqQL

22. https://books2read.com/u/38YKpr

23. https://books2read.com/u/4Dnj6k

Sneak Peak of my next Erotic Fairytale: The Soldier

What if the princess woke up when the Soldier's Tinderbox dog brought her to him?

I woke up to a strange grunting sound that I didn't recognize. I peaked through my eyelashes to determine where the sound came from. A man I had never seen before lay next to me, his eyes squeezed shut in pain or pleasure. I dared opening my eyes a smidge more to look at the rest of him. He was naked and stroking his erection with quick movements. I had to bite my lip to refrain from gasping. It was the first time I've seen a man naked before. Sure I have seen a naked arm, leg and even chest, but I've never laid eyes on a man's member before.

Would it feel hard or soft underneath my fingers? Would it hurt when it entered me? I had so many questions, but seeing that I didn't know him I could hardly ask. I was so engrossed in watching his cock and hands that I almost didn't notice when he reached his release. His groans became louder and I could hear my name mixed in. He knew me, but I didn't know him. My gaze went back up his face, to try to see if I could place him somewhere in my memory. It was hard to determine his age as his face was contorted with pleasure. He didn't have any gray hairs yet, but his face was weathered by the elements and a thick beard covered his cheeks.

His body tensed and with one long groan he reached his climax. I watched in wonder as his cock spurted out his seed, covering his chest and legs in the white substance. I wanted to touch it, taste it, smell it, but I didn't want him to notice I was awake. I quickly closed my eyes before he would see me gawking at his cock.

The Soldier: Erotic Fairytale Retelling - Coming Soon – June 2024